202525

W9-BPJ-706

Published by Oren Village, LLC, Battle Creek, Michigan. For information or
permission to reproduce, please contact author@alanstjean.com or write to
Alan St. Jean, PO Box 1, Battle Creek, Michigan 49016. Text set in Baskerville.
Cover design by Libby Carruth Krock. Illustrations were rendered in
watercolor and pencil.

PUBLISHER'S CATLOGING-IN-PUBLICATION DATA

St. Jean, Alan.

Spooky Mooky / written by Alan St. Jean ; illustrated by Libby
Carruth Krock. -- 1st ed. -- Battle Creek, Mich. : Oren Village, c2008.

p. ; cm.

(The daydreams collection ; v. 2)

ISBN: 978-0-9777272-3-0
Audience: grades K-5.
Summary: Ralphie is afraid of the dark. Something's scratching
at his bedroom window, and there are strange sounds coming from
under his bed. Good thing for Ralphie that his friend, Mooky, isn't
afraid at all.

1. Fear of the dark--Juvenile fiction. 2. Monsters--Juvenile
fiction. 3. Courage--Juvenile fiction. 4. [Fear of the dark--Fiction.
5. Courage--Fiction. 6. Fantasy.] 7. Fantasy fiction. I. Krock, Libby
Carruth. II. Title. III. Series.

Printed in Korea

PZ7.S14245 S66 2008
[Fic]--dc22   0810

For baby Ken.
Grow, live, laugh, and love.

-Alan St. Jean

*

For my mom, Deborah.
Thank you for instilling in me confidence
and strength.

-Libby Carruth Krock

SPOOKY MOOKY

The Daydreams Collection

Volume II

By Alan St. Jean   Illustrated by Libby Carruth Krock

"Don't turn out the light! Not yet!"
Cried Ralphie from his bed.
"The dark is very dark in here,
Let's leave it on instead."
"Ralphie Stump!" exclaimed his mom,
"Your birthday was today.
Eight years old is big enough
To face the dark, I'd say."

"But what about the monsters?"
Ralphie asked, eyes open wide.
"What an imagination!"
Mother laughed, holding her side.
With a great big hug, a kiss on the head,
His mom turned off the light.
She whispered, "Happy Birthday,"
As the darkness met the night.

Ralphie lay back in his bed,
The sheets pulled to his face.
He looked around the room,
In every dark and scary place.
"I'm eight years old," he said aloud,
Which made him feel much better.
"I'm old enough to be a man,
And even wear a sweater."

"I'm old enough to dress myself,
I can tie my shoe.
I'm big enough to reach
The highest shelf and get the glue.
I'm old enough to ride my bike
(With just a little push).
I'm bigger than an octopus.
I'm bigger than a bush!"

Suddenly a tapping sound
Made Ralphie sit upright.
His face turned toward the window,
Then he shut his eyelids tight.
"My bedroom's on the second floor!
Oh, no! Unless it flies,
That monster must be ten feet tall
With teeth, and fourteen eyes!"

A rumble underneath his bed
Made Ralphie jump with fright.
"Something wants to eat me!
Something wants to take a bite!"
Leaning left, and leaning right,
He tried to take a peek.
"That monster may have tentacles,
Might even have a beak!"

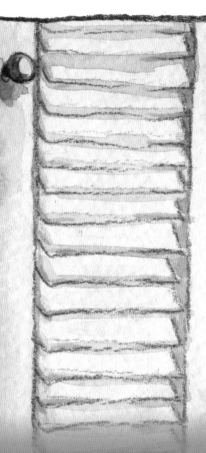

Ralphie heard a swooshing sound
Behind his closet door.
"I should have checked that door before.
I should have closed it more!"
He pulled the sheets atop his head,
"They'll never find me here!
If monsters cannot find me,
Then, there's nothing more to fear!"

Suddenly, another sound.
A squeaky door went *creeeeeak*!
He wondered what had creaked and squeaked,
But Ralphie wouldn't peek.
"The closet monster!" Ralphie yelled,
"He's trying to get out!
With claws and lots of scary teeth,
And lots of hair, no doubt!"

Footsteps, then the sheet pulled back.
His mom turned on the light.
She laughed and hugged him as she said,
"Ralphie, everything's alright.
And, look, you have a visitor!
Mooky from next door.
He couldn't make your party,
So you have one present more!"

Mooky was the neighbor.
He was only six years old.
But he was Ralphie's bestest friend,
Through wind and rain and cold.
He wore a sheet up on his head
That sometimes hid his face.
A Mooky sort of silly thing,
He wore it every place.

Spooky was his nickname,
And 'cause nicknames come in twos,
Spooky Mooky is the name
That all his friends would use.
He wears the sheet to school and church.
He wears it to the park.
It seems he never takes it off,
Not even after dark.

Ralphie's mom went to the door,
Then turned to face the boys.
"You can play a little while,
Show your birthday toys.
But Mooky must be going soon,
It's getting pretty late.
You know, it's still your birthday.
Oh, I can't believe you're eight!"

As the boys began to play,
Again the tapping sound.
"A monster's out my window!"
Ralphie yelled. "Don't turn around!
It's really tall, with fourteen eyes.
We musn't dare to look!
I'm sure it's really hungry,
It might know how to cook!"

Mooky walked across the room,
He touched the window pane.
Ralphie's eyes were bulging
As he clutched his favorite plane.
"Look at all the branches,"
Said Mooky, playfully.
"They're tapping on the window.
As you see, it's just a tree."

A rumble underneath the bed
Made Ralphie tense with fear.
"Watch out!" he said to Mooky,
"There's a monster under here!
It has slimy skin and tentacles.
I think it has a beak.
It might just want to eat us,
So we dare not take a peek."

Mooky lay down on the floor,
Just like an Eagle Scout.
Reaching under Ralphie's bed
He pulled a robot out!
"It's just a toy," said Mooky,
"Lookie here, the switch is ON.
I'll push the switch
from ON to OFF and...
Hey! The rumbling's gone!"

From deep inside the closet
Came the swooshing sound again!
Suddenly the closet door
Opened up, and then...
"Mooky!" Ralphie blurted out,
"Get up off the floor!
A hairy beast with lots of teeth
Is coming out the door!"

Mooky started laughing
As he stood and grabbed the door.
Looking through his sheet, he said,
"I've seen this beast before!
It certainly is hairy.
It's as hairy as a goat.
With zippers for it's teeth,
It looks exactly like your coat!"

Ralphie's head began to bow,
A frown had crossed his face.
Why was he so terrified?
This bedroom was his place.
"Why can't I be brave like you?"
Said Ralphie, feeling small.
"I'm eight years old. You're only six.
But you're not scared at all!"

Spooky Mooky giggled.
"Sometimes I see monsters, too.
But, Ralphie, you're my hero.
I'm not scared when I'm with you!
Here's your birthday present,
But don't open it right now.
I want it to surprise you.
I want you to say, *'WOW'*!"

A happy tear in Ralphie's eye,
He wiped it with his sleeve.
"You're my bestest friend,"
He said as Mooky turned to leave.
"Thank you for my birthday gift!"
Said Ralphy playfully.
"I hope that it's a puppy!
In the morning, we will see!"